Shopkins™

Once you shop...You can't stop!

Mrs. Billings

ALWAYS IN STYLE

By Jenne Simon

SCHOLASTIC INC.

Published by Scholastic Inc., *Publishers since 1920.* SCHOLASTIC and associated logos are trademarks and/or registered trademarks of Scholastic Inc.

The publisher does not have any control over and does not assume any responsibility for author or third-party websites or their content.

Scholastic UK, Coventry, Warwickshire

This book is a work of fiction. Names, characters, places, and incidents are either the product of the author's imagination or are used fictitiously, and any resemblance to actual persons, living or dead, business establishments, events, or locales is entirely coincidental.

ISBN 978-0-545-94059-7

10 9 8 7 6 5 4 3 2 1   16 17 18 19 20

Printed in China

First printing 2016

Book design by Erin McMahon

"Breaking news!" Apple Blossom said. She was reporting live from the Small Mart News Studio.

"World-famous designer Shady Diva is known for her sassy style, great taste, and strong opinions," she continued. "And now the fashion icon is coming to Shopville to look for a new model! She will hold auditions at her Fashion Boutique next week."

Lippy Lips saw the news report. She couldn't believe it!

"Everyone in Shopville knows how much I love fashion," she told her friends. "This is my chance to shine!"

But Toasty Pop did not seem impressed by the news.

"I'm burnt-out on shopping," she said. "But if it's important to you, Lippy, I'll help however I can. Let's get cooking!"

Lippy asked Apple Blossom for her help, too.

"I have to design an amazing new look," said Lippy.

"You *are* a whiz with scissors, needle, and thread," agreed Apple Blossom.

"But what would impress a star like Shady Diva?" Lippy wondered.

Lippy had plenty
of practice creating
styles for her
friends.

Whipping up a
colorful hat would
be easy peasy. And
she could make a
flashy dress worthy
of the runway. Maybe she should design some
jewelry to add sparkle and shine . . .

"I don't know what kind of outfit to choose," Lippy worried.

She knew she would not be the only one in Shopville competing for Shady Diva's attention.

Lippy had seen the camouflage looks that Spilt Milk had been wearing recently.

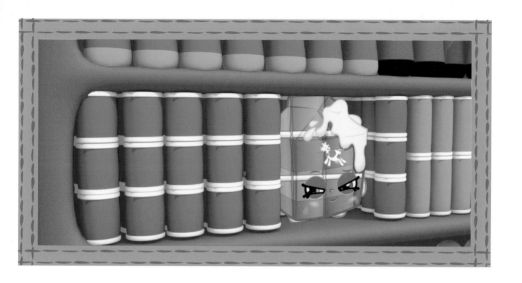

She knew her friend's hidden style would not stay secret for long.

"How can I compete with looks so trendy they seem new every minute?" Lippy wondered.

Dum Mee Mee hoped Shady Diva would design a cute clothing line for the younger Shopkins. She dreamed of baby-blue bloomers with matching rattles.

Kooky Cookie wanted Shady Diva to notice her sweet style. But she was more interested in makeup than clothing.

"I've already chosen eye-shadow colors," she said. "Chocolate Brown, Oatmeal, and Brown Sugar!"

"Brown *is* the new black," agreed Lippy.

Slick Breadstick was sure he'd be the one Shady Diva noticed.

"I have ze perfect hat and ze perfect mustache," he said. "No one can resist zis face."

"The French *do* know fashion." Lippy nodded.

Toasty Pop could see her friend Lippy did not feel confident.

"Just be yourself," she told Lippy. "That's what I always do."

It was true. Toasty sometimes popped her top, but it only made the other Shopkins like her more.

Just then, the Shopville News Team returned with a live update.

"Shady Diva has just arrived in Shopville," Apple Blossom announced. "Her first stop was the Jewelry Store where she proved diamonds really are a girl's best friend."

"And now the famous designer is heading for the Fashion Boutique. Auditions are about to begin!" Apple Blossom said. "Our sources have an eyewitness on the scene."

"Shady Diva's taste in clothes is amazing," gushed Strawberry Kiss. "I bought everything she touched!"

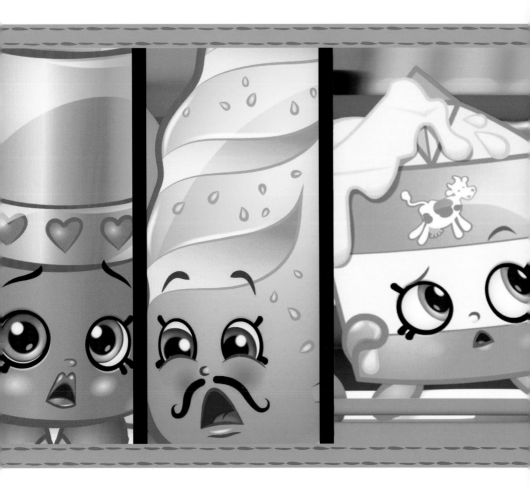

Everyone in Shopville was excited to finally
meet the dashing diva. But they were also a little
scared. Would she think their style was full of
flavor and spice?

And who would she pick as her next model?

The Shopkins dashed out of the Small Mart as quickly as they could.

Everyone wanted to be first in line to meet Shady Diva.

Lippy Lips thought about what she could do to stand out from the crowd as she waited for her turn.

"Color me nervous," she told Toasty Pop.

"Just be yourself," Toasty reminded her.
"Be myself," repeated Lippy. "But . . . who am I?"

Lippy Lips had a colorful personality.
She was the flashiest Shopkin around.
And the best way to shine was with a bit of sparkle!
But which kind of outfit should she choose?

Lippy Lips did not have much time to decide.
Shady Diva had arrived!

Luckily, she knew just what she should do: be
herself!

"Ms. Diva?" Lippy said. "I'll be right back in an outfit that's sure to turn your head."

But Shady Diva did not see Lippy run into the store. She was too busy looking at her next model!

"Who is zis?" Shady asked. "You are hot, hot, hot!"

Toasty Pop blushed. She giggled. And then she popped her top!

"Darlink, you have eet!" Shady told Toasty Pop. "Zat special somezink."

Shady Diva looked Toasty up and down. She inspected her buttons and bread.

"I vill make you a star, darlink," she said. "Your face vill be on the cover of magazines! You vill be my model!"

"I'm not really interested in fashion," Toasty said just as Lippy appeared in the doorway. "You should talk to my friend Lippy Lips. She's got great style!"

Shady Diva studied the outfit Lippy had chosen. It was colorful. And very flashy. And it had lots of sparkle and shine.

"Zis outfit may be a leetle too over-ze-top!" she announced.

"Over the t-t-top?" Lippy stammered.
Her eyes filled with tears.
It hurt to hear that her hero didn't appreciate
her style.

"Don't worry," said Toasty. "You're just being you . . . and that's a good thing!"

Lippy thought about it.

Toasty was right!

Lippy didn't need Shady Diva to make her a fashion star. Especially when she had a friend like Toasty by her side.

"And I can tell everyone *you* were the one to turn her down," Toasty Pop said.

That made Lippy feel even better. She did have her pride, after all.

"I'm glad you're you," said Toasty. "Especially when you're over-the-top."

"I'm glad I'm me, too," said Lippy. "And I'm very glad to have a friend like you!"